The Usborne
Big Book of Machines

Written by Minna Lacey

Illustrated by Gabriele Antonini

Designed by Stephen Wright and Mary Cartwright

Edited by Jane Chisholm and Jenny Tyler

With expert advice from Jon Barrance, Capt. Andrew Douglas, Andrew Gaveed, George Hosford, and Steve Williams

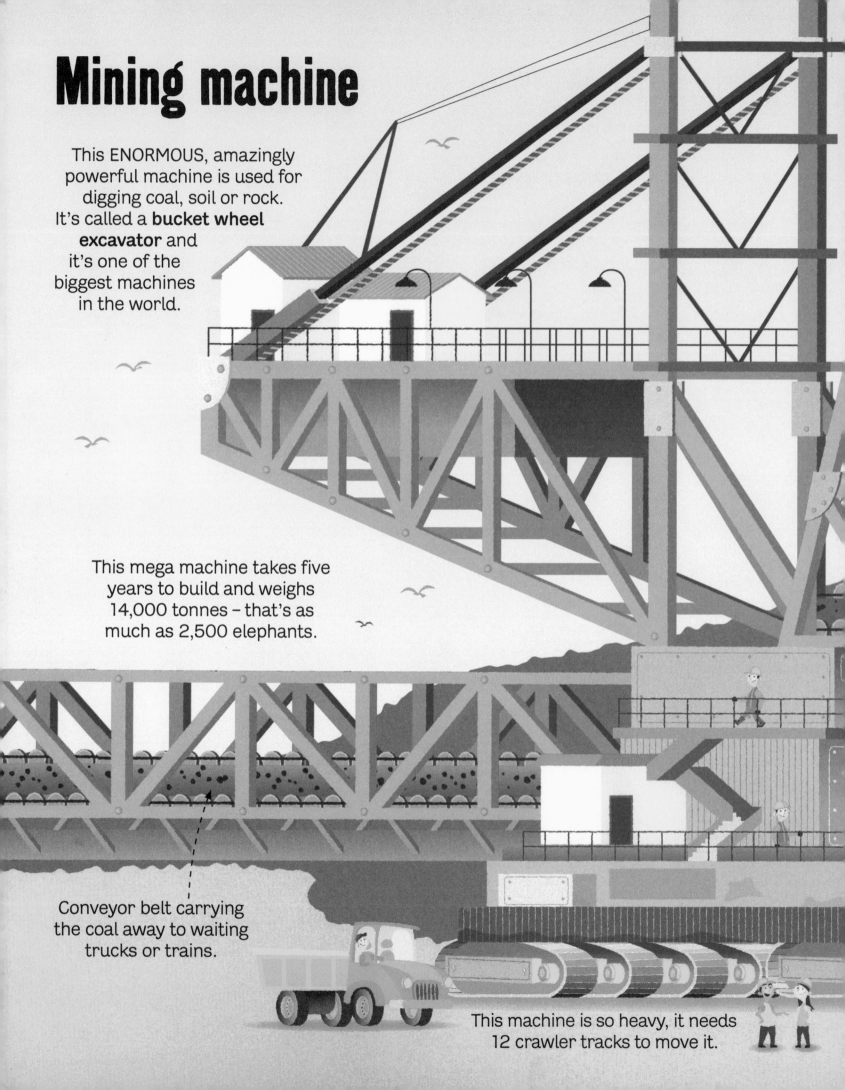

Mining machine

This ENORMOUS, amazingly powerful machine is used for digging coal, soil or rock. It's called a **bucket wheel excavator** and it's one of the biggest machines in the world.

This mega machine takes five years to build and weighs 14,000 tonnes – that's as much as 2,500 elephants.

Conveyor belt carrying the coal away to waiting trucks or trains.

This machine is so heavy, it needs 12 crawler tracks to move it.

Cables to lower or raise the bucket wheel.

The wheel is so HUGE – it's as high as a seven-floor building.

Bucket

Coal falls into the buckets as the wheel turns around.

Bucket wheel

The coal tips out onto a conveyor belt.

Cabin

Empty bucket comes around again.

Buckets with sharp metal scrapers cut into the coal.

Farm machines

A **hedge trimmer** has a flexible arm for cutting hedges.

Maximum reach: 4½ metres – as high as a double decker bus

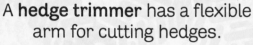

A **quad bike** is handy for driving over rough ground.

A **telescopic handler** has a boom that slides out to lift things.

Lifting height: 6½ metres – as high as a two-floor house

A **combine harvester** cuts crops and separates the grains from the stalks.

Cutting speed: 300,000 stalks a minute

A **baler** wraps hay and straw into round bales and ties them with twine.

Speed: over 300 bales a day

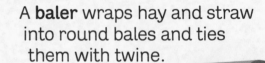
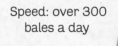

Bale

This HUGE **tractor** can pull very heavy farm machines.

Weight: as heavy as eight ordinary tractors

Lift the pages to see some of these machines at work.

A **crop sprayer** sprays pesticides over the crops to stop diseases.

A **potato harvester** digs potatoes out of the ground

Harvesting speed: 15,000 kilos of potatoes every hour

A **plough** breaks up and turns the earth, to prepare it for sowing seeds.

A **muck spreader** pours animal muck or dung over the fields to help crops grow.

Carries enough muck to spread over two fields.

A **seed drill** plants seeds in neat rows in the soil.

A **disc harrow** breaks up the soil and smooths it for sowing seeds.

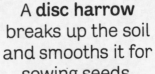

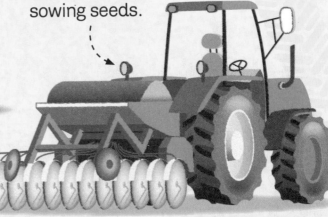

A **bean harvesting machine** picks pods from green bean plants.

Harvesting speed: 8,000 kilos of green beans an hour

Flying machines

The **Antonov An-225** is a MASSIVE cargo plane – the biggest aircraft in the world. It was built to carry a space shuttle on its back.

Tail fin

This man is spraying the plane with de-icing fluid to remove snow and ice.

The **Mil Mi-26** is an amazingly powerful helicopter. It can carry an army tank that weighs 20 tonnes.

Its body is 34 metres long – nearly half the length of a jumbo jet.

This **de-icing vehicle** has a long arm – so it can reach the top of a plane.

There are three SUPER-powerful engines below each wing.

The main landing gear has 28 wheels, 14 on each side.

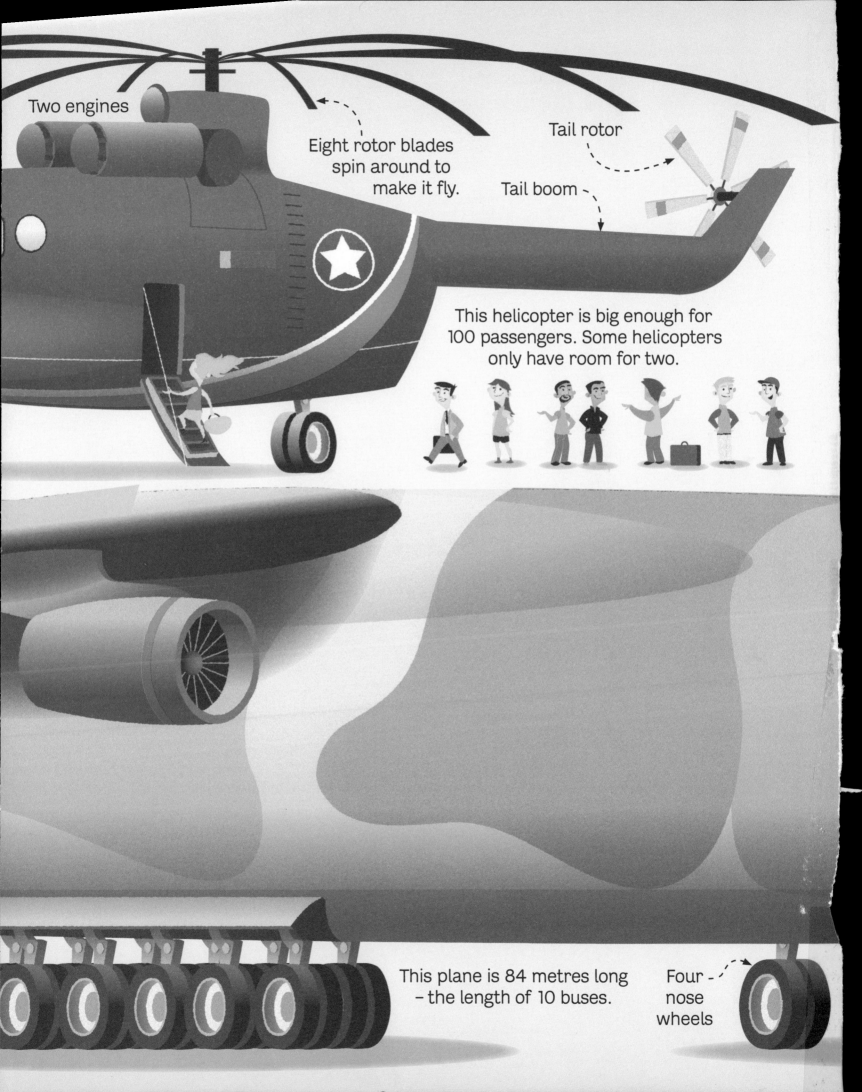

Two engines

Eight rotor blades
spin around to
make it fly.

Tail rotor

Tail boom

This helicopter is big enough for
100 passengers. Some helicopters
only have room for two.

This plane is 84 metres long
– the length of 10 buses.

Four
nose
wheels

This SUPER-SIZED truck weighs more than 200 tonnes – that's as much as 36 elephants.

Each car is chained to the deck to stop it from slipping.

The load is poured or blown in by hose through here.

This **truck** is used for mining. It's SO HUGE and HEAVY that it can't be driven on normal roads without damaging them.

To spread out its weight, it's carried on two **low loaders** travelling side by side.

Its wheels are 3½ metres high. That's almost as tall as an elephant.

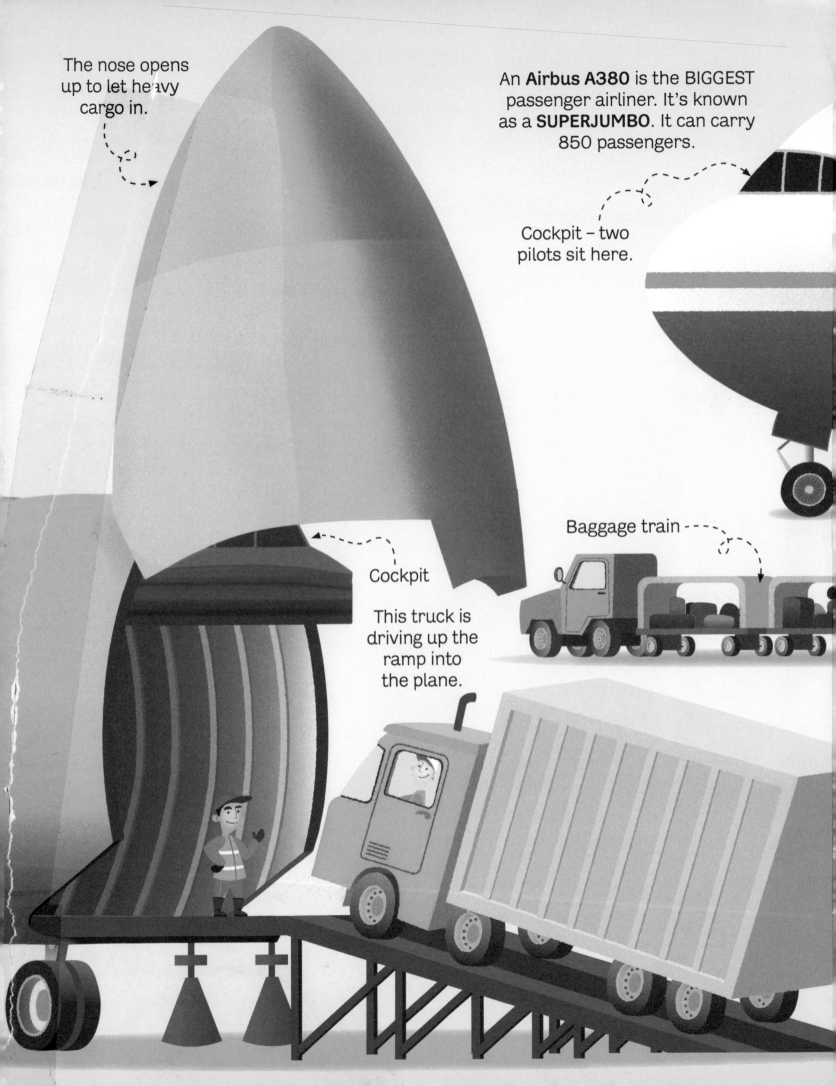

The nose opens up to let heavy cargo in.

An **Airbus A380** is the BIGGEST passenger airliner. It's known as a **SUPERJUMBO**. It can carry 850 passengers.

Cockpit – two pilots sit here.

Cockpit

This truck is driving up the ramp into the plane.

Baggage train

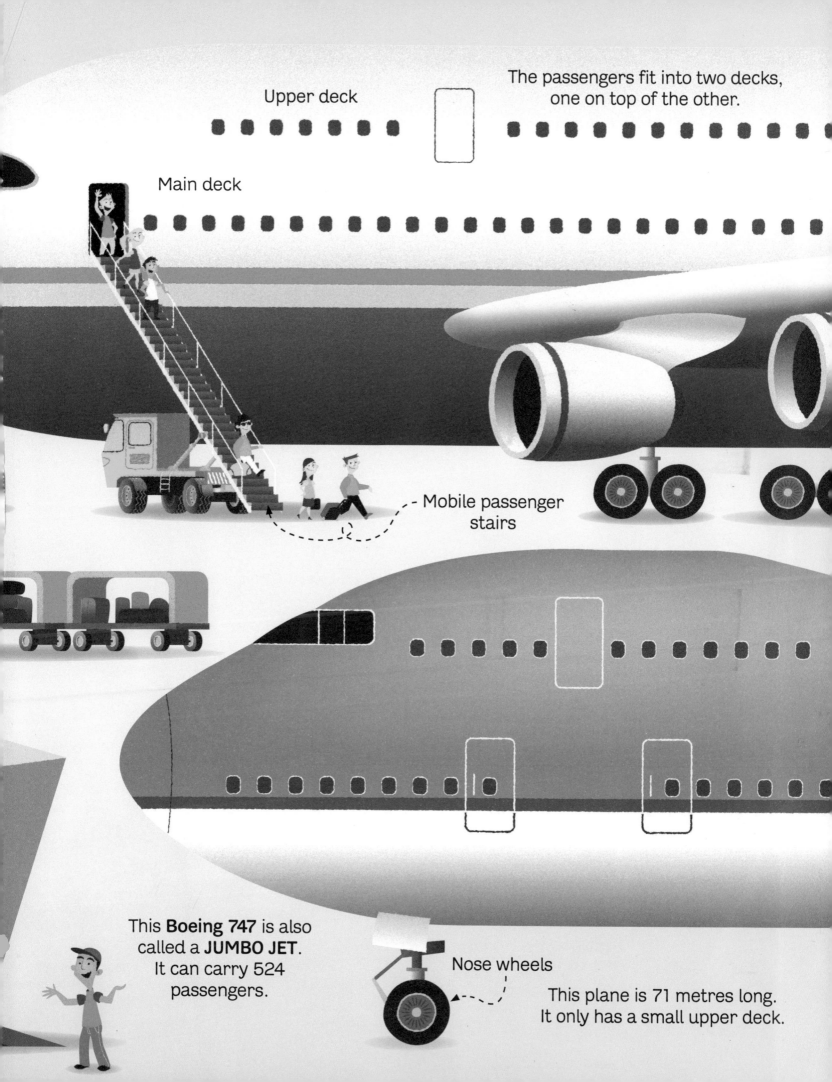

Upper deck

The passengers fit into two decks, one on top of the other.

Main deck

Mobile passenger stairs

This **Boeing 747** is also called a **JUMBO JET**. It can carry 524 passengers.

Nose wheels

This plane is 71 metres long. It only has a small upper deck.

Road machines

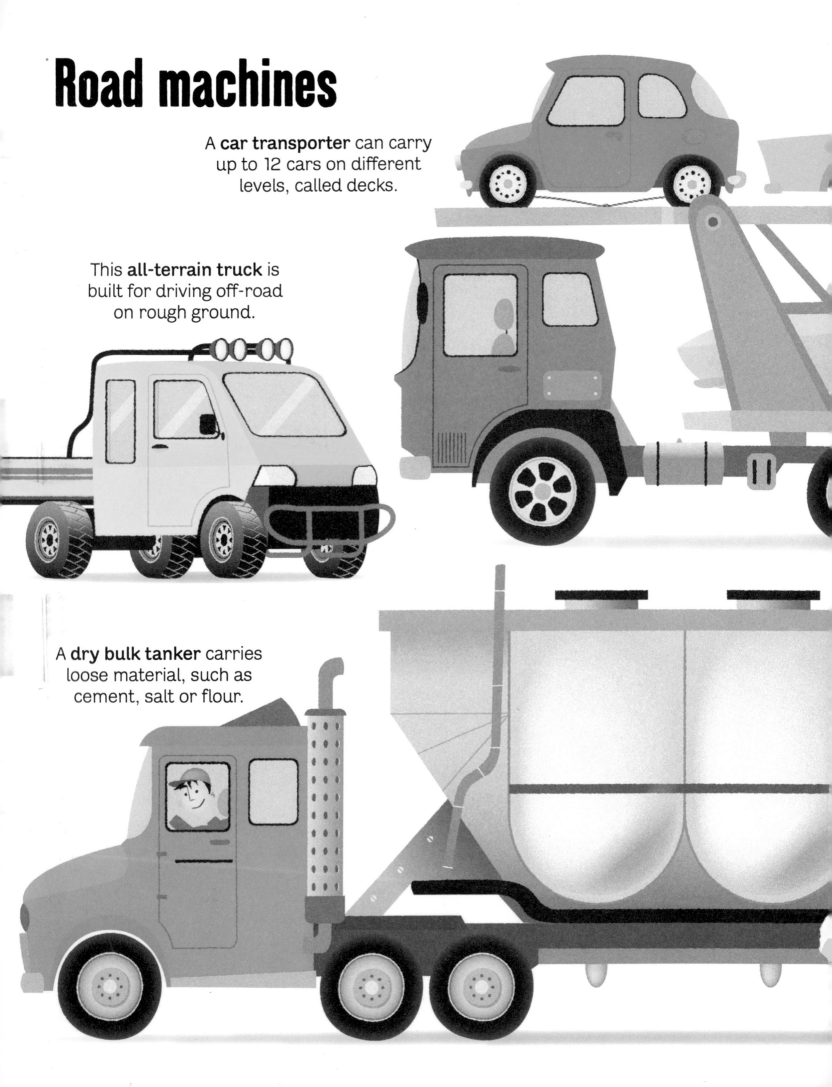

A **car transporter** can carry up to 12 cars on different levels, called decks.

This **all-terrain truck** is built for driving off-road on rough ground.

A **dry bulk tanker** carries loose material, such as cement, salt or flour.

Loader bucket

A **backhoe loader** can dig holes at the back with its backhoe and lift things at the front with its bucket.

Backhoe

A **piling rig** hammers heavy posts, called piles, into the ground.

An **excavator** digs big holes in the ground.

Maximum digging depth: 5 metres – the same as the height of a giraffe

Bucket

Drum

A **pipe layer** places pipes in the ground for water, oil or gas. Each pipe can weigh as much as four elephants.

Pipe

Concrete mixers mix up concrete in a spinning drum.

Drum speed: 20 turns a minute

A **mobile crane** is fixed to the top of a truck, so it can travel quickly between different jobs.

Lift the pages to discover some of these machines at work.

Dockside machines

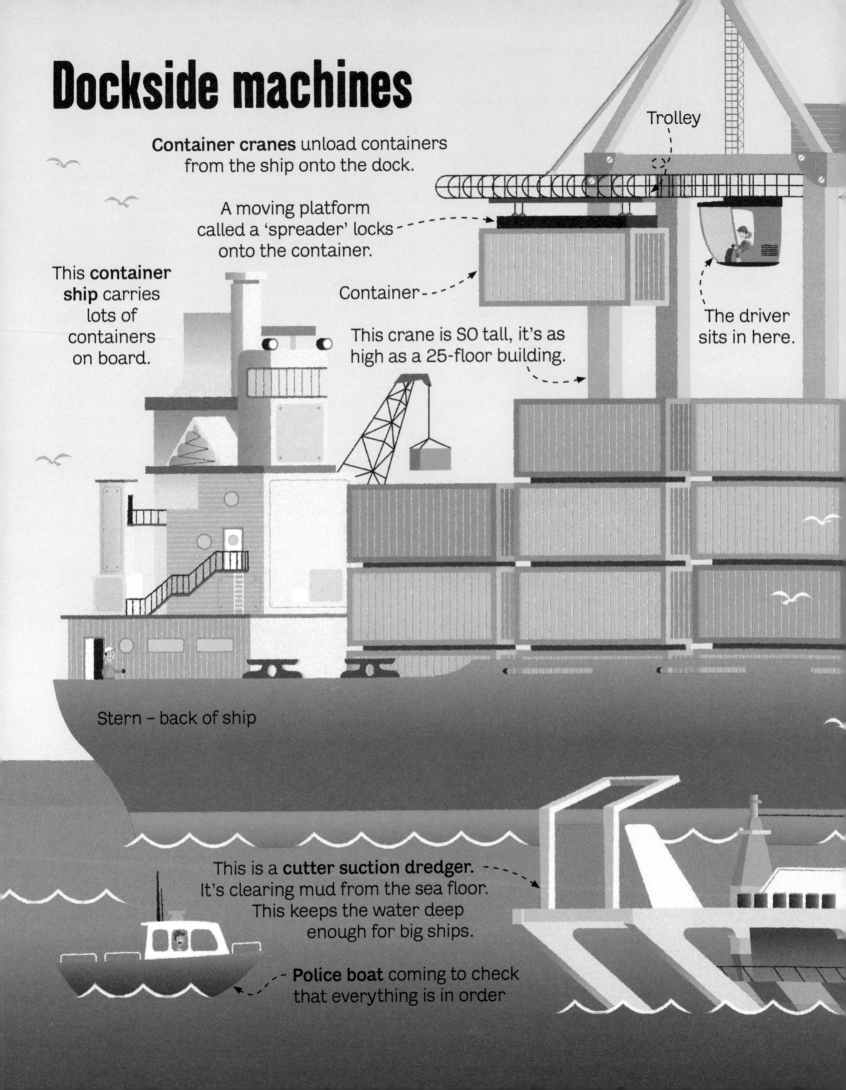

Container cranes unload containers from the ship onto the dock.

Trolley

A moving platform called a 'spreader' locks onto the container.

This **container ship** carries lots of containers on board.

Container

This crane is SO tall, it's as high as a 25-floor building.

The driver sits in here.

Stern – back of ship

This is a **cutter suction dredger.** It's clearing mud from the sea floor. This keeps the water deep enough for big ships.

Police boat coming to check that everything is in order